THE SEMINOLES

BY CHARLOTTE WILCOX

CONSULTANTS: BRENT R. WEISMAN
PROFESSOR OF ANTHROPOLOGY AT THE UNIVERSITY OF SOUTH FLORIDA

LOUISE GOPHER, DIRECTOR OF EDUCATION,
SEMINOLE TRIBE OF FLORIDA

WILLIE JOHNS, CULTURAL EDUCATION PROGRAM,
SEMINOLE TRIBE OF FLORIDA

LERNER PUBLICATIONS COMPANY
MINNEAPOLIS

ABOUT THE COVER IMAGE: The pattern on this fabric is a good example of the traditional patchwork designs created by Seminole women.

PHOTO ACKNOWLEDGMENTS:
The images in this book are used with the permission of: © Dorothy Downs, pp. 1, 3, 4, 18, 27, 37, 45; Historical Museum of Southern Florida, pp. 5, 21, 30, 38; National Anthropological Archives, Smithsonian Institution/1063-W, p. 6; Library of Congress, pp. 7 [LC-USZ62-367], 13 [U.S. Serial Set, Number 4015, 56th Congress, 1st Session, pages 748-749], 14 [LC-USZCN4-147], 32 [LC-USZ62-101151], 33 [LC-USZ62-104529], 34 [LC-USZ62-126400]; © Marilyn "Angel" Wynn/Nativestock.com, pp. 8, 16; Florida State Archives, pp. 9, 15, 17, 28, 29, 40; UT Institute of Texan Cultures at San Antonio, 072-0050, p. 10; © North Wind Picture Archives, p. 11; Woolaroc Museum, Bartlesville, OK, p. 20; Jack Hillers, C. W. Kirk Collection, "Courtesy of the Oklahoma Historical Society," #8823, p. 23; © SuperStock, Inc./SuperStock, p. 24; D. C. Constant Jr. Collection, "Courtesy of the Oklahoma Historical Society," #1456, p. 26; © Bettmann/CORBIS, pp. 31, 47; Western History Collection, University of Oklahoma Library, p. 35; © Hulton-Deutsch Collection/CORBIS, p. 36; © Index Stock Imagery/Willie Hill Jr., p. 39; © Francis Miller/Time Life Pictures/Getty Images, pp. 41, 43; © CORBIS, p. 44; © AP/Wide World Photos, pp. 46, 48; C. R. Cowen, C. R. Cowen Collection, "Courtesy of the Oklahoma Historical Society," #19687.IT.RE.97.14.30, p. 49; Maps by Laura Westlund, pp. 12, 19. Cover: © Dorothy Downs (front and back).

Lerner Publications Company
A division of Lerner Publishing Group
241 First Avenue North
Minneapolis, MN 55401 U.S.A.

Website address: www.lernerbooks.com

Library of Congress Cataloging-in-Publication Data

Wilcox, Charlotte.
    The Seminoles / by Charlotte Wilcox.
        p.   cm. — (Native American histories)
    Includes bibliographical references and index.
    ISBN-13: 978-0-8225-2848-7 (lib. bdg. : alk. Paper)
    ISBN-10: 0-8225-2848-7 (lib. bdg. : alk. Paper)
    1. Seminole Indians—History—Juvenile literature. 2. Seminole Indians—
Social life and customs—Juvenile literature. I. Title. II. Series.
    E99.S28W55 2007
    975.9004'973859—dc22   2005005650

Manufactured in the United States of America
1 2 3 4 5 6 – BP – 12 11 10 09 08 07

CONTENTS

CHAPTER 1

A FREE PEOPLE

ANCESTORS OF THE SEMINOLES

lived across the southeastern United States for thousands of years. Many different tribes existed. Each tribe spoke its own form of a language called Muskogee. Nearly half a million people spoke Muskogee around A.D. 1500.

The life of the Muskogee-speaking peoples was based on related family groups called clans. Clans had names such as Bear or Deer.

Marriage within the same clan was not allowed. When a couple married, the man moved to his wife's clan camp. Children belonged to their mother's clan.

The Muskogee raised crops, hunted for game, and fished. They believed the Creator, or Great Spirit, protected them through spiritual leaders called medicine men. Medicine men used healing arts to help people when they got sick. These arts included medicines made from plants and other natural elements, chants, and songs.

Native Americans used every part of the animals they hunted. Hides were stretched and dried and used for clothing and shelter.

Many tribes held council meetings to form laws, solve disputes, and discuss other issues.

Each tribe had clan elders to govern it. They met together in groups called councils to make rules for the tribe. Some elders inherited their positions from their parents. The councils chose others because of their outstanding wisdom or talent. Tribe members went to the council with disagreements. The council made a decision, and the tribe members had to follow it. The council also had authority to punish those who broke the rules.

EUROPEANS ARRIVE

Starting in the 1500s, many people from both England and Spain entered Muskogee territory.

During this time, many battles occurred between Native Americans and European soldiers. The soldiers killed many Native Americans and took others as slaves. Europeans also spread diseases that killed more American Indians than the fighting did.

Muskogee villages were near creeks, so English colonists called them Creek Indians. Some Muskogees left their homeland to escape the colonists. They moved from their land in what is now Georgia into northern Florida.

When Europeans arrived in Florida, they found many Native Americans living in villages similar to the one pictured below.

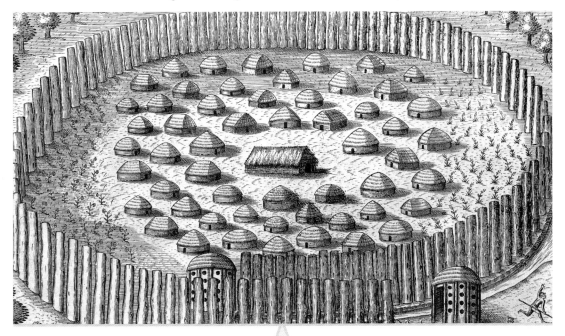

The Spanish colonists living there called them *cimarrón*, which means "untamed." The Muskogees in Florida adopted the Spanish word as their name. In their language, the word became *siminoli*. To them, the word also meant "untamed." They were untamed, or free, because Europeans had never ruled them. English people started calling them Seminoles in the 1760s.

Through most of the 1700s, the Seminole Indians lived quiet lives in many areas of Florida.

In the 1700s, Florida's Seminoles hunted, fished, and otherwise enjoyed a quiet life.

These beaded sashes are from the Brighton Reservation in Florida. Beadwork is an important Seminole tradition.

They had little contact with other native people but traded animal skins, crops, and other foods with the European colonists. Meanwhile, Spain, France, and Great Britain fought over Florida. Many battles occurred, and over the years, each of the countries controlled parts of Florida.

THE SEMINOLE WARS

In 1813, war broke out between U.S. soldiers and Muskogees in Alabama, then part of Mississippi Territory. The fighting was over land claims between Native Americans and white settlers.

Thousands of Muskogees lost their homes. Many escaped to Florida and joined the Seminoles. The Seminoles' peaceful life soon changed again. Many people living in the southern states held African American slaves. Some slaves from Georgia and Alabama escaped and found their way to Florida. They became black Seminoles.

When white slave owners tried to get their black slaves back, fighting broke out. The United States Army invaded Spanish Florida.

Gopher John *(left)*, a black Seminole, was an interpreter for U.S. troops who were fighting his own people.

U.S. troops capture two Seminole men in Florida in 1816.

That started the First Seminole War (1817–1818). The Seminoles and the Spanish fought back, but in 1821, Spain gave up Florida to the United States.

The United States opened Florida to American settlers. The settlers forced the Seminoles off their land in northern Florida. The United States signed an agreement giving the Seminoles land farther south. By then, the Seminole nation had grown to about five thousand people. They were made up of people whose ancestors were Seminoles and other Muskogee-speaking peoples as well as Lower Creeks.

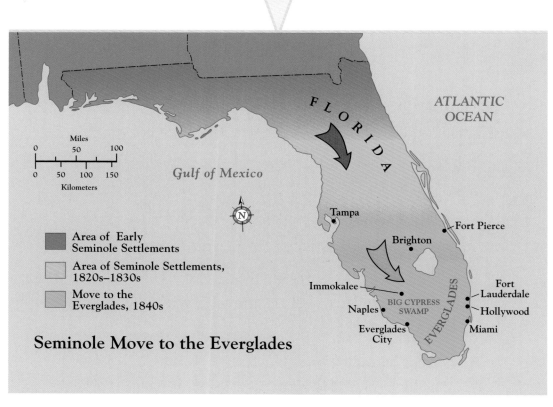

The Seminoles' move to the Everglades

THE INDIAN REMOVAL ACT

In 1830, while Andrew Jackson was president, Congress passed the Indian Removal Act. This law allowed the U.S. government to give land in the West to Native American tribes living in the eastern United States. This land, mostly in Oklahoma, was called the Indian Territory. To receive land, the tribes had to give up their land in the East.

The law stated that the tribes had a choice about moving west. But that is not how it worked out.

Several tribes, including the Seminoles, were tricked or forced into giving up their homelands.

In 1832, the United States sent government officials to Florida. They pressured Seminole chiefs to sign an agreement giving up all Seminole land in Florida. The Seminoles had three years to move to Oklahoma. They would receive land in the Indian Territory but had to share it with other Muskogee tribes.

The Seminoles signed this agreement *(pictured in part, below)* with the U.S. government in Florida in 1832.

MORE WAR

The agreement was not clear about when the three-year term would start. That caused a misunderstanding over what year the Seminoles had to leave Florida. Besides that, many Seminoles refused to leave. This led to the Second Seminole War (1835–1842).

OSCEOLA (ca. 1804–1838) was a mighty Seminole warrior in the Seminole wars. In 1837, the U.S. Army invited Osceola to a peace talk, but it was a trick. With a flag of peace flying, Osceola, along with other warriors, was captured and put in prison. Osceola died in prison in 1838. He was one of the most famous Native Americans of his day. His death was reported in newspapers all over the world.

The Second Seminole War lasted seven years.
The United States lost nearly fifteen hundred
soldiers in the war and spent about $40 million.
About three thousand Seminoles were driven
from their homeland to the Indian Territory.
Most went up the Mississippi River by boat. Then
they traveled overland to the Indian Territory.

Forced from their Florida homeland, many Seminoles
traveled by boat to the Indian Territory.

During the Seminole Wars, many Seminoles escaped to the Everglades, a large, swampy area in southern Florida. Many plants grow there, including saw grass. It grows twelve feet high and has sharp, jagged edges. Alligators, snakes, fish, herons, pelicans, and deer live there.

About three hundred Seminoles refused to leave. They moved deep into the dangerous Big Cypress swamp and a place called the Everglades at the bottom tip of Florida. The U.S. soldiers followed them. But soon the soldiers just gave up.

Peace lasted until 1855. At that time, United States Army scouts entered the Everglades looking for a medicine man called Abiaka. Seminole warriors, led by Billy Bowlegs, attacked.

This started the Third Seminole War (1855–1858). By then, the army decided there were not enough Seminoles to worry about. They left them in the Everglades. The Seminoles remained a free people.

BILLY BOWLEGS (ca. 1810–ca. 1864) Billy Bowlegs was a talented tribal leader. Unlike most Indian chiefs, he spoke English. Many white people thought that Billy Bowlegs represented all Seminoles. After the Second Seminole War, the U.S. government still tried to convince the Seminoles to move west to the Indian Territory. Government agents took Billy to Washington, D.C. There, he met President Millard Fillmore. But Billy and his people still would not agree to move west. Finally, Billy was forced to move. Many of his people followed. Others refused. They remained in the Everglades.

CHAPTER 2

LIFE IN THE INDIAN TERRITORY

IN FLORIDA, THE SEMINOLES REMEMBERED only dishonesty and greed from white people. In the Indian Territory, Seminoles met some white people who were kind and caring. For example, a white doctor, John F. Brown, accompanied Seminoles traveling the Trail of Tears. He was a Presbyterian Christian who was born in Scotland.

Dr. Brown showed great care for the suffering Seminoles. Along the way, he fell in love with a Seminole girl, Lucy Greybeard. They were married in Oklahoma. Dr. Brown spent his life treating the sick in the Indian Territory.

NOT AN EASY LIFE

The Seminoles who moved to Oklahoma faced much trouble. Florida has forests and water. Oklahoma is dry, and much of it is treeless. It gets cold and snows in Oklahoma but almost never in Florida.

On the march west, many Seminoles made the trip overland. Others went by boat to New Orleans, then up the Mississippi River. From there, they traveled overland on foot.

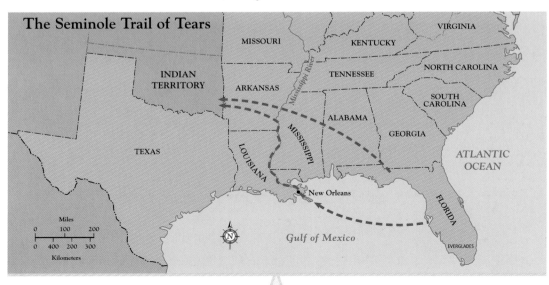

The Seminole Trail of Tears

The U.S. Army forced Seminoles and thousands of other Native Americans to travel almost one thousand miles to the Indian Territory. Many became sick, and many died during the difficult journey.

Other Native American tribes living in the Indian Territory did not welcome the Seminoles. The U.S. government ordered the Seminoles to move onto land already given to the Creek Indians. The Creeks did not want Seminoles on their land. The Seminoles did not want to be ruled by Creeks.

In 1856, the government gave the Seminoles their own land. Seminole land was a strip between the north and south forks of the Canadian River.

It stretched from central Oklahoma to the western edge of the territory. At last, Seminole families could build houses and plant crops. Led by Chief John Jumper, they started to rebuild their nation. But this peaceful life lasted only five years.

DIVIDED AGAIN

The U.S. Civil War (1861–1865) started over the issue of slavery. People in the southern states owned slaves. People in the northern states thought slavery was wrong. They wanted the slaves to be set free. As in many other communities, bitter disagreement divided the Seminole Nation.

John Jumper was born in Florida about 1820. He was a hero of the Second Seminole War. With other Native Americans, he was forced to move to the Indian Territory in 1843. There, he served as the beloved chief of the Oklahoma Seminoles for thirty-one years.

Seminoles were allowed by U.S. law and their own traditions to own slaves. That is one reason that many Oklahoma Seminoles, including Chief John Jumper, sided with the Confederate South in the Civil War. Jumper became an officer in the Confederate army. He led a group of American Indian and white soldiers during the war. Many Seminole slaves became tribal members.

Nearly one thousand Oklahoma Seminoles voted to side with the North, known as the Union. Chief John Chupco, a black Seminole, led the Union supporters.

ALICE BROWN DAVIS (1852–1935) was a daughter of Dr. John F. Brown and Lucy Greybeard Brown. In 1922 Alice became the first woman chairman of the Seminole Nation of Oklahoma. She was a school teacher, interpreter for Native Americans in court, and a missionary to Seminoles in Florida. Alice and her husband, George Davis, raised eleven children. They owned a trading post. She died in 1935.

John Chupco, photographed in the late 1860s.

Seminole land was in the path of the Confederate army as it pushed northward. Chupco's group believed they would be attacked if they stayed in Oklahoma. They joined a group of Creeks trying to reach Union territory. About six thousand men, women, and children left for Kansas in early November.

The journey north was hard. Many died from cold and starvation. A group of Confederate soldiers that included Native Americans attacked on November 19, 1861. Chupco and his party fought them off. Confederate forces attacked Chupco's group two more times before they reached Kansas.

When the Union won the Civil War, it took over rule of the entire South, including Oklahoma. The Seminole Nation of Oklahoma was still divided. The U.S. government recognized Chupco as chief of the Oklahoma Seminoles, but most of the tribe followed Jumper.

BUILDING A NEW NATION

Everything changed in Oklahoma after the Civil War. Native Americans, African Americans, and white people had all lost families, homes, and farms.

The, dry, treeless prairies of Oklahoma were in sharp contrast to the lush homeland the Seminoles knew in Florida.

The U.S. government ordered the Oklahoma Seminoles to free all their slaves and give them tribal rights. The Seminoles had to make peace among their two groups and among other Native Americans.

The government ordered the Oklahoma Seminoles to sign a treaty selling all their land to the United States. The government wanted to open this land to white settlers. The treaty allowed the Seminoles to buy land from the Creeks, so the Seminoles bought two hundred thousand acres of land in central Oklahoma. They had no choice.

The Seminoles worked hard to build a new life in Oklahoma. They built houses and barns, put up fences, and planted crops. By 1870, many Seminoles had become successful ranchers.

BAD DEAL

When the U.S. government forced the Oklahoma Seminoles to sell their land, it paid them only fifteen cents for each acre. When they bought land from the Creeks, the Seminoles had to pay fifty cents for each acre. That is more than three times what the government had paid the Seminoles!

This Council House was built in the 1870s. It was the first one the Seminoles built in the Indian Territory. The tribal council met here.

With just over twenty-one hundred people, the Seminoles owned two thousand horses, four thousand head of cattle, and eight thousand hogs. They had their own police and court system. They built roads, schools, churches, and trading posts.

In 1872, the Oklahoma Seminoles held an election in their capital city, Wewoka, Oklahoma. The two running for chief, Chupco and Jumper, stood in the middle of the main street. Voters stood in line behind the person they supported. Jumper had more voters in his line, so he was elected chief.

CHAPTER 3

LIFE IN THE EVERGLADES

THE SEMINOLES WHO REMAINED in the Florida Everglades also faced many challenges and sorrows. Life in the swampy Big Cypress and Everglades was different from what they had known in northern Florida. In the Everglades, the Seminoles created a new lifestyle. Living in the swamp was not easy. Snakes and alligators were always prowling. Mosquitoes carried diseases and discomfort. Hurricanes came without warning and destroyed whole villages. These were problems, but they also helped keep white settlers away.

The chickee provided protection from the hot sun, heavy rains, and high water. Before settlers came, Seminoles lived in log cabins.

After the arrival of settlers, the Florida Seminoles had to move often. They needed houses they could build quickly. They invented the chickee. The chickee had no walls. Log posts held a wood floor above the ground and held up a roof of palm leaves.

FARMING AND FOODS

The Florida Seminoles raised corn, pumpkins, squash, potatoes, and beans. They also raised sugarcane, bananas, and many other fruits.

Native Everglades plants also provided food. The Seminoles learned to make a flour called arrowroot from the roots of the coontie, a small evergreen bush. The plant had to be cleaned well before cooking and serving it. The Seminoles also cooked swamp cabbage, called hearts of palm, from the cabbage palm.

Every Seminole family had a pot of *sofkee* cooking over their campfire. Sofkee is a drink. The Seminoles made sofkee from corn, rice, grits, or flour and seasoned it with a pinch of fine, white ashes.

A Seminole family enjoys sofkee at dinner in the Florida Everglades. Sofkee is a traditional drink.

Sometimes they made sofkee by boiling tomatoes and guava, a type of fruit. Then they added sugar.

Sofkee was served at every meal. In between meals, people helped themselves to sofkee whenever they were thirsty.

Florida Seminoles hunted deer, wild turkeys, and other birds for meat. They hunted alligators for their skins and raccoons for their fur. They traded the skins and furs to white traders for things such as cloth, coffee, gunpowder, and beads.

Seminole children in Florida learn the traditional skill of using bows to shoot arrows.

When possible, Seminole hunters used an early type of gun with a long barrel. When gunpowder was in short supply, the Seminoles hunted with bows and arrows. They also used bows and arrows when they did not want to make noise with guns.

SEMINOLE CLOTHING

Early Seminoles wore the clothing of their Muskogee relatives. This included common Native American items such as leather moccasins. It also included some European styles such as shirts made of cotton or wool.

A young Seminole woman, Agnes Cypress, shows off a colorful skirt. It is made in the traditional style of Seminole women.

The Florida Seminoles took pride in their appearance. Both men and women liked brightly colored and decorated clothing. They made most of their clothing from cotton or wool. Their favorite material was calico, a cotton cloth printed with colorful flowers and other patterns.

Women wore long, cotton skirts with blouses, capes, and many strands of beads. Seminole women considered beads their most important decoration. Men wore cotton shirts reaching to their thighs, with a belt around the waist.

This photograph was taken in the early 1900s. It shows the traditional clothing of Seminole men.

For special occasions, men wore belts decorated with silver or beads. Every man also had a long shirt, usually made of cotton. It was decorated with cloth ruffles around the edges. Seminole men wore the long shirt during cool weather and for special occasions.

BEADS, BEADS, AND MORE BEADS

Most women spent any extra money they had on beads. They strung them into long ropes. Every morning, a Seminole woman wrapped the beads around her neck, from chin to shoulders. Then she tied the ropes of beads together with small pieces of string to form a large collar. Seminole women often went about their daily work wearing more than ten pounds of beads! Every night, the women cut the small strings to remove the bead collar.

Seminole men wore turbans made of strips of cloth wrapped around the head. The most popular turban style was plaid wool. Paisley and flower prints of wool or silk were also used. Feathers usually topped the turban.

TRADING WITH THE WHITES

The Seminoles had to get their cloth and other items from white traders. Seminole families paddled fifty miles or more by canoe to trading posts.

Seminole men, women, and children ride in canoes on the Miami River in Florida.

The Seminoles in Florida traveled a long way to get to a trading post, such as the one shown here.

They were located at Miami, Fort Lauderdale, Big Cypress, and Everglades City. Seminoles brought their deer and alligator skins, feathers, arrowroot, and other treasures from the Everglades. They returned home with salt, guns, shells, metal items, and rolls of cloth.

In the late 1800s, a few white Christian missionaries, white traders, and government workers started traveling into the Everglades. The rest of Florida was booming with settlers.

Interest in the Everglades began to increase. Vegetable and fruit farms grew up where wild land once was.

The Seminoles lost more and more of their Florida hunting land. Many had to quit their hunting life and get jobs working for white settlers. Some worked on the very farms that displaced their hunting lands.

Other Florida Seminoles worked at tourist shows that staged alligator wrestling. Seminole

These Seminole men learn alligator wrestling for the tourist shows in Florida.

Basket making has been part of Seminole culture for hundreds of years. Many baskets are woven from cane or palmetto. The basket shown here is a coiled basket made from sweetgrass.

women sold crafts to tourists. They learned to make beautiful baskets from sweetgrass, and these quickly became popular items.

In the late 1800s, a new tool arrived at Florida trading posts. Hand-cranked sewing machines changed the lives of Seminole women. By the early 1900s, every Seminole camp had at least one sewing machine. Sewing machines allowed Seminole women to decorate their clothing in new ways.

The introduction of the hand-cranked sewing machine made a huge difference in the lives of Seminole women. It enabled them to make beautiful patchwork designs for their clothing.

One of these new ways was called patchwork. This type of sewing uses small patches or strips of cloth of different colors and shapes. Seminole women sewed the patches and strips together to make borders and ruffles around the edges of clothing.

By the 1920s, Seminole women were expert in making beautiful clothing with patchwork decoration. Their patchwork became works of art. Many patchwork patterns were pictures showing Seminole beliefs. Others were just decoration. Popular patterns included clan names, trees, or everyday events such as fire, lightning, or rain.

CHANGING BELIEFS

About the same time, Seminole Christians from Oklahoma went as missionaries to Florida. They explained to the Florida Seminoles why they had become Christians. A head medicine man of Florida left tribal beliefs to become a Christian in 1920. He and his family helped start the First Seminole Indian Baptist Church. Soon many more Florida Seminoles became Christians. As a result, Seminole Christian churches are located in both Florida and Oklahoma.

Some Seminoles became Christians in the late 1800s and early 1900s. The First Seminole Indian Baptist Church, located in Hollywood, Florida, was built in 1936.

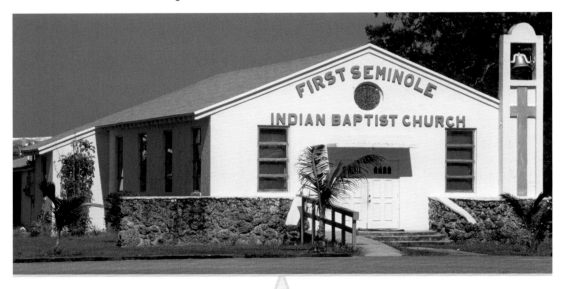

But Seminoles still respect the traditions of their ancestors. They carry on the clan names and stories of ancient times. Seminole medicine men and women still use ancient practices carried down from their relatives. They do not speak about these practices to other people.

The 1900s also brought changing attitudes toward Native Americans. The U.S. government no longer saw them as a threat. In 1928, the government put a road, the Tamiami Trail, right through the Florida Everglades.

The Tamiami Trail runs through the Everglades and the Big Cypress National Preserve.

This family is in a traditional chickee, a style of house designed by the Florida Seminoles.

The trail went from Miami on the eastern coast of Florida to Naples on the western coast. Other roads were built in the 1930s. These roads brought the Seminoles into contact with white people more than ever.

In the 1930s, the government provided more than eighty thousand acres of land for Seminole reservations in Florida. A reservation is land set aside by the government for a Native American group. At first, few moved there.

The Seminoles of Florida had not forgotten the suffering that the Seminole wars caused their ancestors. Florida Seminoles did not trust whites. They did not trust the U.S. government.

In 1934, Congress recognized Native Americans' right to hold their own elections and set up their own governments. But the Seminoles did not want any part of a government that resembled white ways.

Still, a few Florida Seminoles moved out of the deep swamp onto the reservations. They raised cattle, as their ancestors had done. Their move brought a renewed interest among the tribe in managing their own lands.

THE COUNCIL OAK

An old oak tree stands on the Seminole reservation at Hollywood, Florida. Called the Council Oak, it holds special meaning for the Florida Seminoles. At this spot, wise and daring Seminole leaders began to meet to move their people toward a modern way of life. These leaders were the children of the last generation of Seminoles to hide in the swamps. They took bold steps to bring the Seminoles out of fear and need. The Council Oak stands as a living reminder of their work.

In the 1940s, new Seminole leaders arose in Florida. They recognized that fear and distrust were enemies of their people. They realized that hiding in the swamp was no longer the path to freedom. They believed that the Seminoles could enter the modern world as free people and have better lives.

By the 1950s, more than thirty families were raising cattle on the Big Cypress Reservation. Cattle ranching remains an important business on the Brighton and Big Cypress reservations.

Seminole Indians round up a herd of cattle on the Big Cypress Reservation in Cypress, Florida, in 1949.

On July 21, 1957, the Seminole Tribe of Florida voted to adopt a modern constitution. They set up their own independent government. Gradually the Florida Seminoles entered modern life, but the changes were not easy. Both the Seminoles and whites held onto some of the fear and distrust they learned from their ancestors.

Two small groups of Florida Seminoles did not join the Seminole Tribe in 1957. The Miccosukee Tribe of Florida has its own reservation and government. Other Florida Seminoles chose to be independent. They do not belong to either tribe.

Two Seminoles vote on a constitution for the Seminole tribe at the Dania Reservation (later known as the Hollywood Reservation). The election was held in Hollywood, Florida, in 1957.

CHAPTER 4

COMING TOGETHER

IN THE 1950s, the Seminole Tribe sued the U.S. government for payment for land. The government had taken Seminole land one hundred years earlier. In 1970, the U.S. government finally awarded the Seminole people more than $12 million to pay for that land. This marked the beginning of the Seminoles' financial independence.

This Seminole Indian casino was built in Immokalee, Florida, in 1994. It has a bingo hall as well as other casino gambling.

The Florida Seminoles were among the first Native Americans to use their tribal independence in business. In 1977, they opened a store selling tax-free tobacco products. Because the Seminole tribe is an independent government, it does not have to charge taxes as U.S. stores do.

The Seminoles were the first tribe to open a gambling casino. These businesses are called Indian gaming. It is the biggest source of income for Native Americans.

The income makes tribal members self-sufficient. Everyone gets a monthly payment.

The Seminole Water Commission makes rules for water use on reservations. Keeping enough clean water in the Everglades is important in the fight to save endangered species. These are animal or plant families that are in danger of dying out.

THREE NATIONS

The Seminoles of the twenty-first century are actually three nations—the Seminole tribe of Oklahoma and the Seminole and Miccosukee tribes of Florida. They share the same history and many common ties. They work together to improve their lives and solve problems.

This is a version of the seal of the Oklahoma tribe of the Seminole Nation.

Seminole medicine man Bobby Henry is singing a song on Sullivan's Island, South Carolina. He is taking part in a ceremony to honor Seminole chief Osceola, who is buried on the island.

When the Florida tribe learned that the government was going to dig up an Indian burial site in Oklahoma, they sent tribal members. Together the Florida and Oklahoma Seminoles convinced the government not to dig up the graves. But the tribes are also separated by strong differences.

The Seminoles of Oklahoma speak a Creek dialect. They have about twelve thousand members. More than seven thousand live on or near reservations in Seminole County. Another four thousand live in other parts of Oklahoma.

They work in many different professions. These include ranching, business, trades, and the arts.

In Florida, most Seminoles speak the Miccosukee dialect. About three thousand Seminoles live on six reservations. These are at Immokalee, Big Cypress, Brighton, Hollywood, Tampa, and Fort Pierce. They have a successful economy that includes farming, manufacturing, tourism, and gaming.

ENOCH KELLY HANEY (b. 1940) is a famous Seminole sculptor. His sculptures have been shown around the world. He is also a businessperson and member of the Oklahoma State Legislature. One of Haney's most famous statues, *The Guardian*, is of a Native American warrior. It stands atop the Oklahoma State Capitol dome in Oklahoma City.

The Miccosukees have a reservation along the Tamiami Trail. They speak Hitchatee, a form of the Muskogee language. But they claim to have a different tribal history and remain a separate tribe.

The Seminole people are a free people. They govern three nations within the borders of the United States.

THE GREEN CORN DANCE

Every year in late May or early June, Seminoles gather for the four-day Green Corn Dance ceremony. A medicine man determines the exact date. For many years, this has been an important tribal event. Outsiders rarely attend the Green Corn Dance. Seminoles meet with other members of their clan. They tell stories, talk, make music, play ball games, and observe cultural and religious practices. At dusk, a medicine man lights the sacred fire in the middle of the dance circle. Dancers move in a single line behind a medicine man. The men repeat chants while the women make rhythm sounds by tying rattles to their legs. The dancing continues all through the night. Everyone wears beautiful, new clothes as a sign of renewal.

HOW TO MAKE SOFKEE

Traditional sofkee is made with hominy, which is corn soaked in lye. This recipe uses rice and baking powder to get a similar result.

4 cups water
1 cup rice
1 teaspoon baking powder

1. Bring the water to a boil in a medium pot.
2. Stir in rice.
3. After the water returns to a boil, keep it boiling for 12 minutes. Stir it often enough to keep the rice from sticking to the pan.
4. Lower the heat and stir in the baking powder. Keep stirring every few minutes until the rice is tender.
5. Remove from heat. Serve when the sofkee is cool.

PLACES TO VISIT

Ah-Tah-Thi-Ki Museum
HC-61, Box 21-A
Clewiston, FL 33440
(863) 902-1113
http://www.seminoletribe.com/museum

Five Civilized Tribes Museum
Agency Hill, Honor Heights Drive
Muskogee, OK 74401
(918) 683-1701
http://www.fivetribes.org

National Hall of Fame for Famous American Indians
Highway 62 E
Anadarko, OK 73005
(405) 247-5555

National Museum of the American Indian
Fourth Street and Independence Avenue SW
Washington, DC 20560
(202) 633-1000
http://www.nmai.si.edu

Seminole Nation Museum and Historical Society
524 South Wewoka Avenue
Wewoka, OK 74884
(405) 257-5580
http://www.wewoka.com/museum.htm

Seminole Okalee Village and Museum
5716 Seminole Way
Fort Lauderdale, FL 33314
(954) 797-5552 or (954) 797-5553

GLOSSARY

ancestors: family members who lived long ago and from whom others are descended

chants: sayings or songs repeated over and over again

civilized: often to refer to a society with an orderly government

clans: groups of families from the same relatives

descendants: people who come from the same direct line of ancestors

generation: all the people born at about the same time

hurricanes: strong storms with high winds that usually involve heavy rains

medicine man: a spiritual leader who uses healing arts

missionary: someone sent by a church or religious group to teach that group's faith to another people

palm: a tree that grows in warm areas and has a tall trunk with a bunch of large leaves at the top

pastors: ministers or priests who are in charge of a church

patchwork: the process of sewing pieces of cloth of different colors together to make designs

prairie: an area of grassland with few or no trees

sculptor: an artist who creates carvings or statues

swamp: a wet area where some of the ground is covered with water

trading post: a place where things are bought, sold, or traded

tradition: a practice, idea, or belief that is handed down from one age to the next

warrior: someone who knows how to fight battles; a soldier

FURTHER READING

Furstinger, Nancy. *Everglades: The Largest Marsh in the United States*. New York: Weigl Publishers, 2002.

Jumper, Betty Mae, and Peter Gallagher. *Legends of the Seminoles*. Sarasota, FL: Pineapple Press, 1998.

Kavasch, E. Barrie. *Seminole Children and Elders Talk Together*. New York: PowerKids Press, 1999.

Kudlinski, Kathleen V., and James Watling. *Night Bird: A Story of the Seminole Indians*. New York: Puffin Books, 1995.

Sneve, Virginia Driving Hawk. *The Seminoles*. New York: Holiday House, 1994.

Yacowitz, Caryn. *Seminole Indians*. Chicago: Heinemann Library, 2003.

WEBSITES

Everglades National Park
http://www.nps.gov/ever/
The National Park Service website has information about the Everglades plus a large kids' section with activities, games, and coloring sheets.

The Miccosukee Tribe of Indians of Florida
http://www.miccosukeetribe.com/tribe.html
The official website of the Miccosukee Tribe of Indians of Florida includes information about the tribe's history, its leaders, modern-day affairs, and places to visit.

Seminole Nation of Oklahoma
http://www.cowboy.net/native/old-seminole-old/
The official website of the Seminole Nation of Oklahoma contains history about the Seminoles in Oklahoma and modern-day information about the tribe.

The Seminole Tribe of Florida
http://www.seminoletribe.com
The official website of the Seminole Tribe of Florida is very colorful, with plenty of photos and text about history, culture, shopping, and things to do.

SELECTED BIBLIOGRAPHY

Downs, Dorothy. *Art of the Florida Seminole and Miccosukee Indians.* Gainesville: University Press of Florida, 1995.

"The Indian Removal Act of 1830." *Old Sturbridge Village Online Resource Library.* N.d. http://www.osv.org/learning/DocumentViewer.php?DocID =153 (June 30, 2005).

"Treaty with the Seminole, 1832" in *Indian Affairs: Laws and Treaties.* Vol. 2. Washington, DC: Government Printing Office, 1904. Also available online at http://digital.library.okstate.edu/kappler/Vol2/ treaties/sem0344.htm (June 30, 2005).

Weisman, Brent R. *Unconquered People.* Gainesville: University Press of Florida, 1999.

Wickman, Patricia. "The History of the Seminole People of Florida." *The Seminole Tribune,* November 7, 2003.

————. *Osceola's Legacy.* Tuscaloosa: University of Alabama Press, 1991.

————. *The Tree That Bends.* Tuscaloosa: University of Alabama Press, 1999.

INDEX